ERIKA TAMAR

Donnatalee

A MERMAID ADVENTURE

ILLUSTRATED BY

Barbara Lambase

HARCOURT BRACE & COMPANY

San Diego   New York   London

Everyone's out on the fire escapes on
the hottest day of the year. Below me,
Grand Street is steaming. The crowds on the
sidewalk look damp. Daddy tells Mom to put
lunch in a brown paper bag. We're going to
the beach!

We ride the subway to the last stop. Then we have to change to a bus. It rattles, rumbles, and shakes all the way.

My little brothers might get carsick. I don't care how
long it takes as long as we reach the beach.

We snake around bright-colored
blankets, past a jumble of radios
playing all different tunes. I smell
coconut oil and barbecue. I'm afraid
I might step on somebody's head.
The beach is like Grand Street
on sand. Finally we find a spot, a dot
in the Sunday crowd. My brothers
want to eat now. I run to the sea.

I like to sit where the sand is dark and
the water freezes my toes. I squeeze in next
to big wading legs and wait for a roaring wave.
I hold my breath, ready for the shock. The
wave crashes to shore, smashing, splashing,
tasting salty and bitter green.

Foam runs through my fingers. The wave rushes back, pulling and tugging at me. I don't need three wishes; I have only one: to float along with its flow. The undertow's swirl makes me dizzy—it's calling me.

If I love a fish with all my heart, my legs will disappear. I'll have a shimmering tail of blue and green scales. I'll flip it and silently slip into the sea.

I'll have long mermaid hair.

My name will be Donnatalee.

If I swim with a goldfish, he'll take me
home to a castle made of gold. I'll see its
turrets and spires shine from miles away.
I'll have a room all my own. We'll eat from
golden plates. Whatever we touch will gleam.

If I follow a needlefish, he'll string me a mussel-shell necklace. If I want another, he'll thread mother-of-pearl. He'll stitch up a fishnet coat as light as the foam. It will trail behind as I glide through the endless space of the deep.

If I go with a blowfish, we'll blow bubbles and horns. We'll celebrate all night long. There are no neighbors to bang on the pipes if we laugh or sing too loud. We'll dance to the rhythm of the tide, under waving streamers of seaweed.

From far away, I hear Daddy's voice. "Kate! Where are you? Come here." I'll send him a letter in a bottle. It will wash up on shore. I'll write, *Don't worry about me. I'm where I belong. Love from Donnatalee.*

If I stay with a swordfish, we'll always be ready for duels. Danger will make us laugh. We'll chase the looping sharks away from scared little fish. We won't let monsters sneak into our ocean at night. We'll stand guard on the coral reef.

If I ride with a sea horse, we'll be wild and free. There'll be no red lights to make us stop and no one to get in the way. We'll gallop over currents of stormy froth. We'll race with the lightning. We'll speed through vast stretches of aquamarine.

If my fish friend asks, "Do you love only me?"
I have to say the truth: "What I love most is the sea."
Then King Neptune will claim me for his own.

We'll dive into bottomless emerald pools. My blood
will turn to green water and salt. I'll drift with him and
be his queen, forever Donnatalee.

"Kate," Daddy calls, "come on, time to go!"
My pail is heavy with shells. The subway is
crowded. More people squeeze on as it jolts
to each stop. I'm itchy. I'm gritty and hot.
I have to sit still, next to a fat lady's thigh. I'm
scrunched with my brothers in only one seat.

I wait my turn for the shower. My shoulders burn in the spray. Sand collects at the drain, and I watch it circle and disappear. There's sand left in my sneakers. I won't ever shake it out. Sand in my shoes means I'll return to the sea.

Under my eyelids, it's deep-water dark. My white cotton nightgown is cool to my skin. I'm tide-washed and sun-dried down to the bone. Inside, I'm bleached clean by the sea.

I press my best shell against my ear. The creaks of the bunkbed over my head and the blasts of car horns outside fade away. I hear Neptune's voice calling. I smell sunshine, salt, and bitter seaweed. Again, I am Donnatalee.

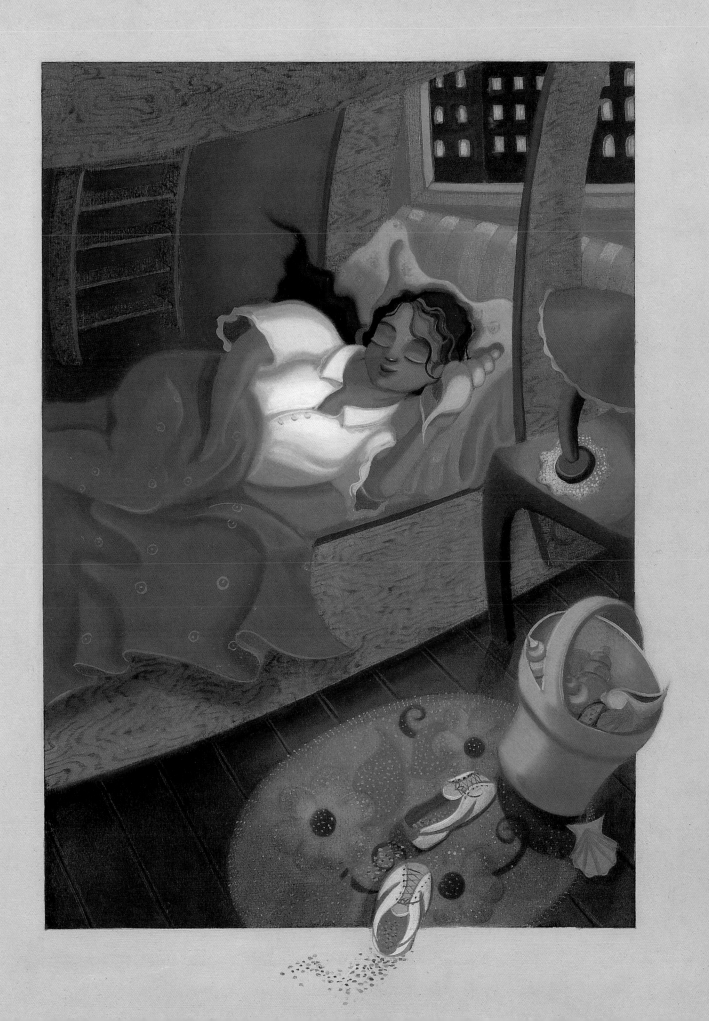